ANNA AND THE TOOTH FAIRY

BY
MAUREEN WRIGHT

ILLUSTRATED BY
ANNA CHERNYSHOVA

SCHOLASTIC INC.

*With love to my forty-plus nieces/nephews
and grandnieces/nephews, from Aunt Mo*
—M. W.

For my sister, who has always believed in me
—A. C.

ISBN 978-1-338-28085-2

Text copyright © 2017 by Maureen Wright. Illustrations copyright © 2017 by Anna Chernyshova. Published in the United States by Amazon Publishing, 2017. This edition made possible under a license arrangement originating with Amazon Publishing, www.apub.com. All rights reserved. Published by Scholastic Inc., 557 Broadway, New York, NY 10012, by arrangement with Amazon Publishing. SCHOLASTIC and associated logos are trademarks and/or registered trademarks of Scholastic Inc.

12 11 10 9 8 7 6 5 4 3 2 1   18 19 20 21 22 23

Printed in the U.S.A.   40

First Scholastic printing, January 2018

The illustrations are rendered in digital media.
Book design by Jen Keenan

The Tooth Fairy will be visiting me soon, so I'm making her a present!

I ask Mom, "What should the Tooth Fairy's dress look like?"
"Pink and frilly, like Sophie's," she says.

Sophie is my baby sister. Babies are okay, but Mom says Sophie is too little to play horsie with me.

"I don't know how to draw a
magic wand," I say.
Sophie waves her sparkly rattle.
"It's a little like Sophie's rattle,"
Mom says.

I add a sparkly wand to my picture.

Mom yawns. "I'm so tired," she says.
"Sophie kept me up all night long."

I wiggle my loose tooth. The Tooth Fairy stays up
all night long, too. She goes around the world collecting
teeth and leaving money under pillows.

Dad comes home and I ride on his back, pretending he is my horse.

Then he picks up Sophie. "Did you get any teeth yet, baby girl?"

Dad says,

"Look, Anna! Your baby sister is flying!"

Tooth Fairies have to learn how to fly, too.

I pick up my Tooth Fairy picture again.
Sophie looks just like the Tooth Fairy.
Mom said Sophie stays up all night.
Dad asked her if she's gotten any teeth yet.
And Sophie is taking flying lessons!

My baby sister must be

training to be a Tooth Fairy!

Maybe Sophie is going to take my tooth when it falls out.
I need to help her as much as I can so that she will be the
best Tooth Fairy ever!

The next day I teach her about money. Tooth Fairies have to know these things.

Sophie likes my painting . . .

so I let her paint along with me.

I tell Sophie that Tooth Fairies have to learn to be very quiet so they can sneak around without anyone hearing them.

Tooth Fairies also like sparkly things!

Tooth Fairies have to get used to the dark.
I gallop over to Sophie with a baby blanket
and toss it over her head. Sophie kicks her
little feet and laughs.

Even though she can't play horsie,
my baby sister is more fun than I thought!

Before dinner I ask Mom, "Can a Tooth Fairy leave her job to come play with me during the day?"

"No," says Mom. "She's way too busy to do that."

Oh no! That means Sophie's going to leave me when she starts being a Tooth Fairy.

The next morning I get an idea. I'll make sure that I don't lose my tooth. Then my little sister won't have to start her Tooth Fairy job!

I try using a bandage to keep my tooth in place. It doesn't stick.

I use a pretty scarf to keep my mouth closed. Sophie pulls it off.

Now my tooth
is even more

Wiggly!

Every time my tongue touches my tooth, I feel it wobble back and forth. I don't eat any pizza at dinner even though it's my very favorite food.

"Little horses have to eat, too," says Dad.

I shake my head and stomp my foot like a horse.

I keep my mouth shut
when I put on my pajamas
and grab Huckleberry.

Mom comes in with Sophie
and says, "Are you okay?
You're awfully quiet."
I say, "Mmmmm-mmm."

"You do know that it doesn't
hurt to lose a tooth, right?"
I finally open my mouth.
"I know that, but if I lose a tooth
then my little sister will have to
go far away."

"Sophie isn't going anywhere," says Mom.
"She'll always be your little sister."
"She will? Forever and ever?" I ask.

"Yes," says Mom, giving me a hug. "You'll *both* be my girls forever."

Hooray!

I give my very loose tooth a good **wiggle**, and out it pops!

"That's wonderful!" says Mom.

I put my tooth under my pillow.

Mom sets my picture of the Tooth Fairy on the windowsill.

Huckleberry and I stay very still and listen for the Tooth Fairy, but we don't hear a thing.

In the morning my tooth is gone and there are quarters under my pillow!

I run to find Sophie to make sure she hasn't flown away.

I'm so happy to see her!

I kick up my legs like a bucking
bronco. I grin at her and she
smiles right back at me . . .

with her very first tooth!